TEAM HERO

FIGHT FOR THE HIDDEN CITY

ADAM BLADE

ORCHARD

MEET TEAM HERO ...

JACK

POWER: Super-strength

LIKES: Ventura City FC

DISLIKES: Bullies

RUBY

POWER: Fire vision

LIKES: Comic books

DISLIKES: Small spaces

DANNY

POWER: Super-hearing

LIKES: Pizza

DISLIKES: Thunder

... AND THEIR GREATEST ENEMY

GENERAL GORE

POWER: Brilliant warrior

LIKES: Carnage

DISLIKES: Unfaithful minions

CONTENTS

THE ASSEMBLY hall at Hero Academy was the oldest part of the medieval fortress. The walls were solid stone, a metre thick, and huge wooden beams spanned the ceiling. The tapestries and pictures hung on the walls showed battles from the ancient war between Team Hero and the shadow armies of Noxx.

Today, the hall was packed with students from every year. They wore silver bodysuits with coloured shoulder pads to show which house they belonged to. Teachers sat on the raised stage. All eyes were on Chancellor Rex, headmaster of Hero Academy, who stood at the speaker's podium.

No one noticed the two students who entered late, at the back, though they did look an odd pair. One was tall and wiry, walking with a slight stoop; the second was squat, almost as wide as he was tall. If any of the other students had turned and really looked, they might have noticed something weird about the newcomers' faces — their features were completely still, as if frozen in place.

"Students of the Academy," said Chancellor Rex, "thank you for gathering. I know that many of you are worried about your teacher, Ms Steel," he went on. "I'm afraid she is still in a coma, but we are going to try another treatment." A murmur travelled through the hall, and the two odd students at the back looked at each other. Their faces didn't move

though, almost like pictures.

"Ms Steel is being taken to Valour Station, our Team Hero outpost in the Flammara Desert," continued Chancellor Rex. "We hope she will have more chance to recover there."

At that moment, the face of the shorter student flickered and distorted. His taller companion muttered. "Quick, let's get out of here!"

As they hurried back through the doors, Chancellor Rex was still speaking to the assembly. "Some of our newest recruits will be accompanying Ms Steel to Valour Station, to take part in desert training . . ."

The two strange students ran along the corridors. The shorter student's face was blurring, giving brief glimpses of ugly mottled skin beneath. Finally his tall companion bundled him into a bathroom.

As he looked into the mirror, the fake visage was completely gone, revealing his bald head, with thick lips and missing teeth and squinty eyes too close together. "Useless!" said Bulk. "I thought you were supposed to be a great sorcerer."

"It's your horrible sweat interfering with the magic," said the taller student. He waved a hand across his own face and the boy's image disappeared, replaced with sharp features, glowing eyes and pointed teeth. "Still, the glamours could use a little work. You shouldn't have rushed me in copying the faces of those two new students." said Smarm. "On top of wiping their memories, it was impossible for me to do it properly."

"We were lucky to catch them before they reached the Academy in the first place. Can you do it again?" asked Bulk, cheeks quivering. "We can't fail in our mission."

"We already have the information we need," replied his companion.

"We do?" said Bulk, confused.

"Weren't you listening?" said Smarm. "Ms Steel's going to the Flammara Desert, so that's where we go too. She's the perfect vessel for our master, and the spells were almost complete last time. We just have to recapture her."

Bulk grinned. "Easy!" he said.

Smarm wrung his bony hands.

"Perhaps," he said. "And this time, no one will stand in our way. Especially not Jack Beacon."

CHAPTER 1

DESTINATION: KHALEA

THE JET plane knifed through the sky at close to the speed of sound, but Jack barely felt any movement where he sat.

"This is so cool!" said Jack's friend Danny beside him. He tucked back his hair to reveal over-sized, bat-like ears. "The engines are so quiet, even I can barely hear them!"

The students were seated in the back of Arrow, the Hero Academy aircraft. They faced each other in two rows. Jack sat between Danny and Ruby, his best friends at the school. Opposite, an older boy called Olly was with his gang, taking it in turns to scowl or snigger.

"Hey, snake-hands!" said Olly.

For a moment, Jack felt like he was back at his old school in Ventura City. He'd spent years thinking that the strange scaly skin on his hands made him a freak, but he'd recently discovered that his hands gave him incredible strength. That's why he was now a student at Hero Academy — a secret school for the gifted. Every student had a different power. All of them were training to become part of Team Hero, the ancient organisation that protected the world from the evil of the realms at the centre of the earth.

"You think you'll survive Flammara?" said Olly. "It's pretty brutal down there. Over forty degrees in the daytime, below freezing at night."

"We'll manage, thanks," said Jack. "You just look after yourself."

Olly's smirk vanished. "You think

you're special, don't you? Just
because Chancellor Rex thinks you're
the so-called Chosen One!"

"Ignore him," muttered Ruby, her
striking orange eyes flashing. "He's
just jealous."

Chancellor Rex believed Jack was
the answer to an ancient prophecy
— the Chosen One who would save
the human world from the forces of
shadow. The headmaster was even
more convinced of this after Jack had
defeated the evil General Gore in a
one-on-one duel in the underground
kingdom of Noxx itself. Jack and his
friends had also destroyed Gore's

armies of shadow warriors before they could swarm the Earth's surface. Jack had gone from being a zero at his old school in Ventura City, looked down on by everyone, to the saviour of the human race. But deep down, Jack still felt like a normal boy. Sometimes he wondered if he was in some weird dream.

Aside from Olly and his friends, there were a dozen other students on board Arrow. Instead of their usual silver bodysuits with coloured shoulders, everyone was wearing bulky black outfits. One student at the end of the row, a beefy boy who

Jack didn't know, was being noisily sick. His tall, lanky friend shifted away from him on the bench. Jack assumed they must be new students at the Academy. Their faces looked strangely still.

"Can't you keep it in?" the friend said. "It's really disgusting!"

If he really was the large boy's friend, then Jack didn't think he was being very nice to him.

The squat figure vomited again into a bag.

Jack peered towards the cockpit, where Professor Yokata, their teacher, was flicking an array of switches and checking read-outs. Jack would have loved to have a go in the pilot's seat for a few minutes. Rumour had it that Arrow's weapon systems were the most high-tech in existence. If needed, it was a deadly combat craft far in advance of anything the military possessed.

Yokata stood up and turned to them. She too was wearing one of the black outfits. Arrow was artificially intelligent, just like the Oracle devices all the students wore in their ears. The plane could fly itself if needed.

"Up, everyone," said Yokata. She was a slight woman with cropped brown hair but a fierce gaze. Her left eyelid was scarred and slightly closed up, but no one knew when or how she'd received the injury. "We're nearing our destination."

Everyone rose to their feet, and Olly grumbled, "How are we supposed to train in these suits? I can barely walk."

"They aren't combat suits," snapped the Professor. "All will become clear."

Yokata pressed a button, and a door in the floor slid open. A floating med-pod that contained Ms Steel rose up from the cargo area. Jack's stomach twisted. It was a reminder that this was no ordinary training mission.

They were also taking their teacher to
Valour Station, in the hope her health
could be restored. She'd been captured
by Gore's sorcerer, Smarm, who'd been
hoping to use her body as a vessel for
his master's spirit. Jack had prevented

the ritual from completing, but Ms Steel had been seriously hurt by Gore's shadow essence.

It was Ms Steel who'd originally recruited Jack to Hero Academy and she'd always been kind to him. He'd do anything he could to help her recover and drive out the shadow that infected her.

"Lock down for landing," Yokata instructed Arrow, before turning to her students. "Have a look out of the windows."

Clamps rose and latched on to the med-pod, fixing it in place securely. Jack turned to the window closest to him. Clouds scudded past them at incredible speed.

"Activate stealth mode," said the teacher.

Jack's heart thumped and everyone cried out as the wings of the aircraft simply disappeared. Though the wings were gone, their speed seemed to stay the same. Jack thought it must feel a bit like riding inside a bullet.

But how can we stay in the air without wings?

"Don't panic," said Professor Yokata. "Arrow is built from a metal that bends light. When in stealth mode, we can see out, but from the ground the craft is completely invisible."

Jack smiled at the wondrous technology. *Amazing!*

As Arrow began its descent, they dropped below cloud level and the city of Khalea came into view. Jack gasped at the soaring skyscraper spires and domes, the elevated walkways and gleaming buildings — an island of metal and glass in the middle of a vast desert of rolling dunes.

"In approximately thirty seconds, we'll be directly above the Team Hero outpost called Valour Station," said Yokata.

"Is there a runway?" asked Danny.

"You won't be landing," said Yokata with a mischievous smile. "Arrow, jump-hatch."

In the side of the plane, a hatch slid open. Jack felt the tug of swirling currents of wind.

"Training starts now," said Yokata. "Your skysuits' jet-boots are controlled with your leg muscles, and your sleeves have aerofoil fins which act like wings. You can use your Oracles' visors for mapping and guidance. I'll see you at Valour Station."

Their teacher stepped through the hatch and dropped like a stone.

"What?!" said a blonde girl a few

seats down from Jack. "She cannot be serious!"

The large new student looked ready to be sick again.

Jack saw the Professor gliding through the air like a bird of prey.

"No problem," said Olly. "I don't even need a suit for this."

He took off his skysuit to reveal his normal silver uniform below and jumped out, disappearing in a flash.

"Show-off," said Ruby. "Just because flying is his power." She turned to Jack. "Ready?"

Jack nodded. "Let's do it."

"Visor activating," Jack's Oracle said

into his ear.

A plasma screen extended from Jack's earpiece over his eyes. Data scrolled down the side: altitude, speed, oxygen levels. "Thanks, Hawk," said Jack.

Danny looked a little pale as he stared through his own visor at the city, miles below. Jack knew he didn't like heights much.

"Don't worry, you can do this," Jack told his friend.

Danny nodded. "Let's go."

The three friends jumped together.

The wind smashed Jack like a fist and he was suddenly spinning.

Everything was a blur, and several beeping alarms were coming from his suit.

"I'd stabilise, if I were you," said Hawk. *"We're dropping fast."*

"Easy for you to say," said Jack. He straightened his legs, activating his leg boosters, then lifted his arms, fins spreading out underneath them. After a couple of slower spins, he got the hang of things, and steadily propelled himself through the air.

A network of lights flashed an alert across his visor, highlighting an area a few miles from the city. Jack zoomed the display to see a circular

building that looked like four giant stacked pancakes made entirely of mirrored glass. *Valour Station*.

"Now this is fun!" said Ruby, from just above him.

Jack saw her zip past, performing a loop. Danny shot after her, twirling. Above, Arrow became fully invisible as its hatchway closed. Jack felt a jet of air from above, and guessed that the craft had banked sharply, on autopilot. The two new students were darting in chaotic zigzags as they tried to gain control of their skysuits.

"Do you think they're OK?" said Jack, skimming alongside his friends.

"My Oracle just told me that the suits have homing chips," said Ruby. "They'll take over if they get into real trouble."

"Out of my way, losers!"

Jack looked over his shoulder and saw Olly shooting towards them, a sneer on his face. Jack shoved Ruby out of danger, and blasted his own jet boots to get clear. Olly barely missed them as he whipped by.

"Careful," shouted Ruby. "You'll hurt someone."

Olly came to a stop, hovering in the air. "And wouldn't that be a shame?" he said. "Anyway, I'll see you at

37

Valour— Oof!"

The squat new student crashed into Olly from above, hurling him through the air.

"Oops!" the large student said. "Can't get the hang of this at all!"

Jack almost laughed, but then noticed that Olly's limbs were hanging limp as he plummeted for the ground.

"I think he's been knocked unconscious!" said Danny.

Jack wasted no time in flipping over and engaging his jet boots at full power. The force almost took his breath away, but he managed to angle his arm fins and steepened his dive in pursuit of Olly. Valour Station sped towards him.

"Warning," said Hawk. *"At this velocity a collision is likely."*

"Tell me something I don't know," said Jack, through gritted teeth.

"OK," said Hawk. *"If you hit the ground at this speed, your body will reconfigure itself over an area approximately ten metres square."*

"When you say 'reconfigure', you mean 'splat'?"

"Affirmative. Impact expected in eleven seconds."

Olly was falling like a rag doll, but not as fast as Jack. Jack drew up alongside him, wrapping his arms around Olly's waist. They were falling towards Valour Station at fifty metres per second, according to the display on Jack's visor.

"Can my boots support us both?" Jack asked.

"Negative," said Hawk. *"Impact in five seconds."*

Jack kicked out his boots towards the ground and felt like his spine was being crushed as they slowed. Jack tightened his arms around Olly, who flopped against him. The roof of Valour Station approached at horrible speed. *We're not going to stop in time!*

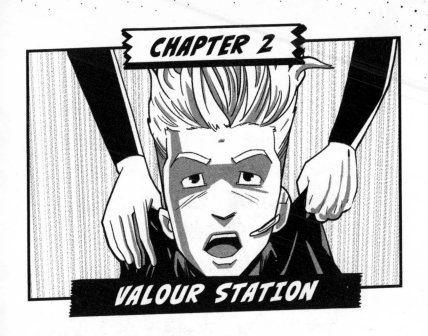

CHAPTER 2

VALOUR STATION

A SECOND before impact, Jack felt
himself yanked upwards as Ruby
and Danny gripped his skysuit at the
shoulders. The three of them and Olly
all landed hard on a metal platform,
crumpling into balls.

Jack rolled over on to his back,
breathing hard.

Olly's eyes were open and he sat up, shaking his head from side to side.

"What happened?" he mumbled.

"You almost got yourself and Jack killed," said Ruby, advancing on him. Olly scooted away. Ruby's special power was shooting fire-beams from her eyes, and for a moment she looked like she was about to use them.

"Leave it, Ruby," said Danny, stepping in front of her. "He shouldn't have been showing off, but it was an accident."

Ruby glared for a second longer at Olly. "You should thank Jack — he saved your life."

Olly blushed, and muttered "Thanks" under his breath. One by one, the other students landed near them on the roof. Even the two odd-shaped ones seemed to have finally got the hang of the suits. Then Arrow came in at a glide, slowed, and descended vertically on down-jets to one of the rooftop landing pads.

Jack saw Khalea City's skyscrapers soaring in the distance. They were impressive, but he thought few looked as grand and as modern as Valour Station.

Professor Yokata came up to the roof by a set of stairs. She had already removed her skysuit to reveal her silver Hero Academy uniform with gold shoulders. She was accompanied by two white-clad scientists, who entered Arrow and then guided Ms Steel's med-pod out. Jack rushed over. "Is everything all right?"

"They're taking Ms Steel to a treatment centre," said Yokata. "She's in the best possible hands now."

"I know," said Jack. "It's just . . . well, Ms Steel was injured rescuing us."

Professor Yokata's face tightened and she looked at him. "Jack, there were many casualties in the fight against General Gore. There always are in war. Ms Steel knew the risks."

Jack was shocked at her cold tone. "But maybe we can help?" he said. "We can tell the doctors exactly what happened at the Noxxian outpost."

"That information is already in your report!" snapped Yokata. "You aren't to go anywhere near Ms Steel, and that's an order. Got it?"

All the other students looked up at the outburst. "Now go to the dorms on Level Two and get some rest. There's some serious training to do tomorrow," finished Professor Yokata.

Jack joined the others, taking an elevator to the second storey of the station.

"I don't like it," he muttered to Danny and Ruby. "The Professor is hiding something."

Once he emerged from the elevator and entered Valour Station itself, Jack realised that the base's mirrored walls were actually tinted one-way glass. The outside reflected most of the harsh desert sun. The rest of the walls were immaculately white, with touchscreens embedded. It couldn't have been more different from Hero Academy, with its ancient stone, vaulted arches and cold draughts!

Hawk directed them through several curved corridors. Jack realised they were staying near to the edge of the circular building. "I wonder what's in the middle," he said to his friends.

"Touch the wall and you'll see," said Hawk.

Jack reached out and did so. A section became transparent to reveal a vast open space beyond, gloomy but lit with spotlights.

"Oh my!" said Ruby.

All the students gathered to look through. Inside Jack saw a huge dig site, reaching deep underground, where ruins were being uncovered. There were several stepped pyramids, collapsed domes, and archways made of huge blocks of pale stone. Here and there he saw the same symbol carved — a circle with lines radiating from it, like a sun.

"Is it an outpost of Noxx?" muttered Danny.

"I don't think so," said Ruby. "Noxx's symbol is a black sun, but that one is different. It almost looks like—"

"What are you kids up to?" barked

a voice behind them.

They all spun round to see two security personnel with energy blasters on their hips.

"We're part of the training group, from Hero Academy," said Ruby.

"Well, the ruins are off-limits," said the guard. He touched the wall again, making it solid. "You'd better be on your way."

"What I was going to say back there," whispered Ruby as they continued to the dorms, "is that I think I've seen that symbol in the library. And I think it has something to do with Solus."

"But Solus is just a myth," said Danny.

"What's Solus?" asked Jack.

"Solus, the lost cities of the sun. According to legend, it's supposed to be an ancient civilisation of four cities, buried in a great sandstorm hundreds of years ago," said Danny.

Jack frowned. "Do you think the ruins are why Valour was built here?"

The other two shrugged.

The dorms were as sleek as the rest of the building — with windows ten metres tall looking out on to the dunes, and floating sleep-pods with touchpads to control temperature and music. Each had a name displayed on the headboard. Danny found his closest to the door and after messing with the touchpad, managed to make it blast out a rock tune. He leapt on to the pod like a surfboard. "We need to get these back at the Academy!"

There were panels on the wall beside every bed, and when Jack waved his hand past one, a desk and wardrobe slid out.

As they got settled, other students drifted into the room and began to get ready for bed. It wasn't long before a series of delicate chimes sounded and the lights around the dorm dimmed. Jack climbed into his pod, which was between Danny and Ruby's. He tried to fall asleep, but didn't feel tired at all.

Ruby sat up in her own pod. "I don't know about you guys," she whispered, "but I don't feel at all sleepy."

"Me neither!" Danny whispered back. "I mean, we just jumped out of a plane!"

"I say we find out what's really going on with Ms Steel," said Jack.

His friends nodded.

They crept back to the door. Danny used his super-hearing to make sure no one was outside. When the coast was clear, they crept out. Jack asked Hawk to find the treatment centre. The Oracle device flicked out a semitransparent visor over Jack's face, projecting a 3D map that showed the building.

"Looks like we go down another floor," Jack said.

They took the fire escape stairwell instead of the elevator, just to avoid being seen, and soon reached the medical centre. Doctors walked about in white coats, typing on tablets. There were X-ray screens, equipment tables and hover-stretchers, as well as some sort of hologram of a skeleton.

"It's the third room on the left," Hawk told Jack.

Jack was careful to avoid the medical staff as he darted for the door with his friends close behind. But as they rounded the door, they found the room vacant apart from a blank monitor and several trailing wires.

"Where is she?" said Danny, wearing a look of concern.

To Jack's surprise, the window was open, and there was already a fine layer of desert sand on the floor. It looked very out of place on the otherwise spotless floor.

Jack stared out over miles and miles of empty desert.

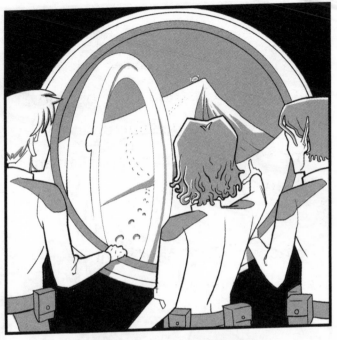

No. Not completely empty. To the south-west were some moving black spots.

"Hawk, magnify," said Jack.

The Oracle extended Jack's visor again. There was no map this time;

instead the distant image became
clearer. Jack's blood ran cold. Two
figures, both dressed in black, were

guiding Ms Steel's med-pod up the side of a massive sand dune. The visor said they were already over a kilometre away.

Jack turned to his friends. "Ms Steel's been kidnapped!"

CHAPTER 3

A HIDDEN CITY

"KESTREL, LOCATE Professor
Yokata," said Ruby to her Oracle.

"The Professor is not on-site," Kestrel
replied. Ruby's Oracle had synched
with Jack's and Danny's so all the
friends could hear. *"She had business
in Khalea City and has requested not to
be disturbed."*

"Who else, then?" said Danny.

Jack frowned. He looked again at the open window. "Someone sneaked in. This was done by an insider. Until we know who we can trust, I say we go alone."

After a brief pause, both his friends nodded.

"But the kidnappers are way ahead," said Ruby. "We can't go on foot."

"Hawk," said Jack. "Are there any vehicles in the station?"

"The Quartermaster's depot is on the ground floor," his Oracle replied.

"Let's see what we can get our hands on," Jack said. "But first we need to get our weapons."

They rushed back to the dorm where Jack retrieved Blaze, his sunsteel blade, Ruby got her mirror shield, and Danny picked up his crossbow. Then they took the stairs down a level, and arrived at a vast hangar filled with equipment. Arrow was docked there, along with several helicopters and desert vehicles with caterpillar treads. Jack led the others behind one, as a group of guards walked past.

"We can't take any of these," said Danny. 'Even if we worked out how to drive it, I'm pretty sure they'd notice."

But Jack had spotted something else: a large cabinet with hoverboards suspended from pegs. "What about those?" he said. They'd trained with something similar back at the Academy. It was mostly a case of good balance.

Once the guards were out of sight, they hurried over. Each took a board and stood on it, strapping their feet in.

Jack pressed the accelerator pedal on the front and turned his back foot to control the height. The board rose up from the ground and zoomed forward. The three of them streaked towards the open bay doors, then

emerged over the desert sands. The sun had dipped beneath the horizon, leaving the sky a dark blue. As they travelled further from the lights of Valour and the city of Khalea, the first stars began to twinkle above.

Jack had lost sight of the kidnappers and Ms Steel, but the dune he'd last seen them on was clear enough — it stretched for miles.

"Hawk, scan for life-signs ahead," he said.

"I'm not picking up anything," said the Oracle.

Jack growled with frustration. Did that mean the kidnappers were too far ahead already?

But soon they found some marks in the sand.

"Footprints!" said Ruby.

"They look more like paw-prints," said Danny uneasily.

Jack let his board skim close and examined the twin trail. Danny was right — the prints were four-toed, with a central pad, like a cat's but much larger. "Perhaps they're wearing shoes adapted for the desert," he said. "That explains how they got away so fast."

They followed the tracks up to the side of the dune and along the base of its slope, for several kilometres. But then the prints suddenly ended.

Jack had a sinking feeling. "The sand must have shifted," he said, turning to his friends and seeing the hopelessness in their faces. "We've lost them."

"Wait!" said Danny. "I think I hear voices." His bat-like ears twitched. "At first I thought they were behind us, but now I think they're coming from inside the sand dune."

"Huh? That's impossible," said Jack.

"Jack, your sword!" cried Ruby.

Jack saw that it was glowing in its scabbard. He drew it out. Guided by some instinct, he pressed the blade against the sloping sand. As it touched, Jack was shocked to see a ray of light burst from the dune. They all leapt back in alarm. It looked as though the sword had ripped a hole in the fabric of the dune.

"The dune is some sort of illusion!" said Ruby, peering closer. "The sand isn't real."

Jack pressed again, then sliced with his sword, opening a larger gash. The light shining out was so bright he couldn't look directly at it, but as his eyes adjusted, he saw more sand on the other side.

"I guess that's where they went,"

said Danny, squinting.

"Well, that's where we follow," said
Jack. He sheathed his sword, and
stepped through the tear.

On the other side, he struggled to

believe what he was seeing. He and

his companions were standing on

the edge of a sandy valley so large

he couldn't see the other side. In the

vast canyon below were four separate

cities arranged around a stepped pyramid similar to the ruins they'd caught a glimpse of at Valour Station. But this pyramid was hundreds of metres tall. A colossal statue stood in the centre of each of the four cities. They were several storeys tall and built from sandstone – a cat, mid-pounce; a falcon with its wings spread and claws outstretched; a cobra rearing back, hood fanning out; and last of all, a scorpion, stinger arching high over its back.

But the strangest thing of all was the dazzling light. It was day here. Hanging high above the pyramid, overlooking all four settlements, was a white ball of light, like a mini sun.

"I don't understand," said Ruby. "How could this place be hidden under a sand dune?"

"The sand dune is just a projection," said Danny. "I think these are the lost cities of Solus. The ruins back at the base must have just been an outpost."

Jack breathed out slowly. A few metres to his right, Jack spotted the kidnappers' tracks again. "Got you!" he said.

They set off on their hoverboards once more, down the steep side of the valley towards the four cities. *Solus.*

Cities of the Sun, Jack marvelled, as they made their way to the pyramid. *I wonder if Team Hero knows about this place.*

The trail of footprints ended at the base of the pyramid. "I guess we go up," said Ruby, craning her neck.

They left the boards at the base and went on foot. The pyramid had gardens and fountains and water channels running around its many levels, though where the water came from wasn't clear. There were doors too — all of them closed. It was hard going, and Jack's legs were aching by the time they neared the top. The strange sun was still way overhead, and filled the sky with pure light.

As Jack stepped on to the pyramid's top level, he was stunned to see hundreds of people gathered there, all wearing strange costumes. Then he realised that they weren't costumes! Speechless, Jack scanned the crowd. All the creatures stood on two legs like people, but some had the furry heads of cats; others had scales and flickering tongues; others had tails ending in bulbous stingers and pincer claws where their hands should have been. The last group had wings, and sharp beaks in their feathered

faces. *Bird-people!* Four different
species, and each similar to the
towering animal statues in the four
surrounding cities.

The only thing they all had in common was that they were looking the same way, to a point directly under the sun, in the centre of the pyramid's flat roof.

There, on a plinth, lay Ms Steel's med-pod.

CHAPTER 4

SOLUS

"WHAT ARE they doing to her?" said Danny.

"I don't know," said Jack, "but it's time we put a stop to it."

He drew his sword. At the sound of the scraping metal, two guards on the edge of the group turned. One was a scorpion-tailed fighter, the other a bird-creature. The scorpion's bulbous tail began to glow.

"Look out!" cried Ruby. She shoved Jack out of the way as a beam of energy shot from the stinger. The bird-

man took off, revealing talons that fizzled with electricity. He folded his wings and dived straight at Danny, who cocked his crossbow, but too slowly.

Jack jumped in, using Blaze to slice at the talons. The bird-creature flapped away, and Jack was left with the tingle of an electric shock.

Several more guards rushed at them — a mixture of all the strange hybrid beings. The snake-soldiers had knotted whips, while the cat-soldiers brandished spears with serrated points. Ruby's eyes fired up, and she blasted a warning arc at the feet of their attackers.

"We don't want to fight!" she shouted.

"Too late for that," muttered a feline soldier. He dropped into a crouch and leaped high into the air, wielding the spear. An energy bolt from Danny's crossbow met him in mid-air, and the creature dropped with a yowl.

Then the others charged.

There are too many, Jack realised at once, as he backed off towards the edge of the pyramid. *But I'm not leaving Ms Steel*.

He lost sight of his teacher as their enemies closed in. Ruby blasted back a couple with a wall of fire, and one of Danny's exploding crossbow bolts flung several aside. Jack lifted his sword above his head, ready to make his final stand . . .

"Cease!" yelled a voice.

The advancing soldiers skidded to a halt.

Jack threw a glance at Danny and Ruby, who looked as surprised as him. The crowd of attackers parted. Through the middle of them walked a cat-like woman wearing flowing robes and a jewel-encrusted headpiece. She carried no weapon. Jack couldn't tear his gaze from her strange green eyes.

Her pupils were vertical slits.

"You wield Blaze, the sunsteel blade," she said softly, "which means you must be the Chosen One."

A gasp went through all the onlookers, but Jack didn't know what to say.

"That's him!" said Danny, nodding enthusiastically. "He's the Chosen One for sure."

"And I am Queen Felina," said the woman, "ruler of the kingdom of Solus. You are welcome here."

"You're in charge?" said Ruby. She nodded nervously at one of the snake-soldiers. "Of everyone?"

Queen Felina smiled. "Though I am one of the Leoriah, I have been elected by the people of all four cities. They are the Herptamon . . ." She pointed

to the snake-head. "The Tavnar . . ."
She indicated a soldier with a scorpion
tail. "And last of all, our feathered
brethren, the Avaretti."

Jack still wasn't sure whether he
could let his guard down. *Why have
they taken Ms Steel?* "My name is
Jack," he said. "And these are my
friends Ruby and Danny."

"I know who you are," said Queen
Felina. "The warrior who defeated
General Gore." She waved a hand at
the soldiers. "Forgive us for reaching
for our weapons. We do not see many
humans here."

"You have one there," said Jack,

pointing Blaze towards his teacher. "What are you doing with her?"

Queen Felina gave a tinkling laugh, but Jack didn't understand what was so funny. "Come," she said, turning and gesturing for him to follow.

Jack and his friends followed the queen towards the med-pod resting on the raised platform. As the ranks of strange hybrid creatures closed in behind them, part of him wondered if this was some sort of trap. When they got close, Jack saw the med-pod was open, and Ms Steel lay on the cushioned surface inside. Her dark features were peaceful, her purple

hair spread out on the pillow. Queen
Felina walked right up to her, and
took Ms Steel's hand in her own.
The queen spoke while gazing at Ms

Steel's face.

"It was my sister who told me about your bravery and that of Team Hero, Jack," she said.

"Your sister?" said Ruby.

Queen Felina reached for the ring on Ms Steel's index finger. Jack had noticed it the first time he met his teacher — a green gem a lot like a cat's eye. As the queen pulled it off, a shimmer passed over Ms Steel, travelling up her arm, then across her body and limbs. Last of all, her face blurred. Gone was the dark skin and purple hair, and in its place was grey fur.

It was all a disguise! thought Jack, looking into the cat-face.

"Ms Steel is one of the Leoriah!" he cried. In the back of his mind, he remembered something Chancellor Rex had once said about Ms Steel being different from the rest of the Team Hero. *This must have been what he meant.*

"That's right," said the queen. She stroked her sister's cheek fondly. "Only we call her Panthera."

"So she was from Solus all along," said Danny. "How did she end up at Hero Academy?"

"We are allies with you," said Queen Felina. "As a civilisation of light, Solus is one of General Gore's ancient enemies. In fact, Panthera was our emissary to Team Hero.

Chancellor Rex knows the truth of her identity, and that's why he sent her to Valour Station, on the doorstep of Solus. He knew that she would have her best chance of recovery here among her own people."

"So you didn't kidnap her," said Jack, blushing. Suddenly he felt rather foolish.

"No," laughed Queen Felina again. "But we had to sneak her away to maintain the secret of Solus."

"The fake dune was clever," said Ruby. "If Jack hadn't had his sword, we'd never have found this place."

"The blade comes from Solus,"
said Queen Felina. "The Sunforge, in
fact. It resides deep in this pyramid,
powered by the Starstone." She
nodded to the huge sun that filled
the sky above them.

This was a lot to take in, but Jack
had other things on his mind.

"Can you help Ms St— I mean,
Panthera?"

Queen Felina looked grave. "I
cannot, but the Starstone might be
able to. Stand back, and we shall
see."

Jack and the others did as she
said, joining the ranks of Solus

citizens a short distance from the med-pod. Queen Felina raised her hands, and Jack saw that an opal jewel in the centre of her crown began to gleam more brightly. She started to chant under her breath — strange words that meant nothing to Jack. Then the Starstone shot a beam of white light straight downwards. It enveloped the pod in a glow so bright he had to shield his eyes.

Suddenly, from behind, there came a number of angry voices. Jack turned as a bolt of dark energy knocked part of the crowd to the ground, in order to make way for two figures. One wore scuffed leather armour, his flesh bulging between the gaps. The other was taller, wearing a brown hooded robe. He seemed to glide behind his clumsy companion.

"It's Bulk and Smarm!" cried Danny.

Jack reached for Blaze, but Bulk charged into him, knocking him into Danny and Ruby. As he hit the ground, he saw something in Smarm's bony hand. A vial, filled with swirling black shadow.

Jack realised at once what it was. *General Gore's essence! They want*

the General to possess Ms Steel's body. They're trying to finish the ritual to resurrect Gore!

"Protect Ms Steel!" he shouted. "Don't let the shadow touch her!"

CHAPTER 5

TIGORA'S RAMPAGE

THE NOXXIAN sorcerer flung the vial of shadow at Ms Steel.

Jack was too far away to help, but Queen Felina was not. She pounced, and her tail lashed at the vial. The small glass jar rebounded and struck the med-pod, exploding. None of the shadows touched Ms Steel, but instead they seemed to be sucked into the beam of light from the Starstone. Tendrils of black began to climb towards the miniature sun like tentacles.

Jack saw Smarm and Bulk already fleeing past the shocked onlookers. Some of the citizens of Solus were backing away as the shadows climbed the beam of light. The dark tendrils spread, moving more and more quickly up towards the glowing orb.

"The Starstone!" Queen Felina cried in horror.

When the
shadows
reached the
Starstone, its
surface began
to blacken.
Jack felt the
air grow cooler,
and a gusting

wind kicked up around them. Queen
Felina's face was twisted with worry.
"I don't think we can stop it!" she
said.

The Starstone's light dimmed a
little as the shadow took grip.

Gore's spirit is infecting it . . .

Gloom set in over the pyramid and a tide of shadow began to travel across the valley below. Jack watched helplessly as it threw the buildings and streets of the Leoriah city into darkness. It reached the huge cat statue, turning the golden surface black.

Then the statue moved.

For a moment, Jack thought his eyes were playing tricks on him, but the gasps of others soon told him that it hadn't been his imagination.

"Tigora!" breathed Queen Felina.

Flakes of stone fell from the cat. Then, like a crumbling sandcastle, the statue collapsed into dust and poured off the pedestal.

"What's happening?" asked Danny.

"Tigora is meant to be our sacred protector from the desert," said the queen. "I don't know what the shadow is doing to her."

"We have to find out," said Jack. "Ruby, can you stay here and guard Ms Steel? Bulk and Smarm might return."

Ruby nodded.

"Danny, follow me!" said Jack.

He and his friend bounded down the steps of the pyramid. Reaching the bottom, they raced into the

Leoriah city, which was made up of simple sandstone buildings, all crowded close together over narrow alleyways. They crossed through several squares with stalls set up selling delicate pottery, jewellery and fine silks in incredible colours. Cat-people were rushing around in panic; some hurried inside the buildings, others pointed up at the Starstone, casting darkness over the once bright city.

At last Jack and Danny reached the empty pedestal of the statue, rising high above the central plaza. Tigora had turned into sand, and the last grains were falling from the platform. Suddenly, the city fell eerily quiet.

Jack turned, holding out the sunsteel blade. "I don't like this," he said.

Danny crouched, and laid his ear close to the ground.

"I hear something," he said.

Then Jack felt it too — a slight vibration through the soles of his feet like a gentle rumble.

"Earthquake?" he said.

Part of the paved plaza burst open with a fountain of sand. Jack almost toppled in shock, and Danny

scrambled to load his crossbow. A
lion-like creature as big as a cow
stood facing them, but instead of fur,

its skin seemed to be stone, its eyes merely hungry hollows. It opened its jaws to reveal jagged fangs and a gaping black throat.

"Er . . . nice kitty," said Danny.

The lion pounced at Jack. Without thinking, he slashed with his sword. As the steel struck, the creature exploded back into a shower of sand.

"Whoa!" said Danny.

They heard a scream, and a young Leoriah child ran into the square, chased by two more of the sand lions. Danny's energy bolt stuck the first, piercing its chest and turning it into a cloud of sand. The second pinned the girl to the ground. It roared and lowered its head to rip her to pieces. Jack hurled Blaze in a spinning arc, exploding the beast. His sword buried itself in the wall of the building behind.

The girl was trembling as Jack helped her to her feet.

"Thank you!" she said, before her cat eyes widened. "You're a human."

Jack nodded. "We're here to help," he said. He turned to see the piles of sand on the ground re-forming into lion shapes. "Uh-oh. We've got a problem. Get inside," he told the girl. "Bar your doors."

The girl scrambled away as the lions became whole once again.

How can we destroy them if they just re-form?

The lions prowled towards them, then the first dropped into a crouch and pounced. Danny fired one of his exploding crossbow bolts at the first lion, shattering it to dust. But as he reached for his quiver to reload, the two others charged him from either side. Jack couldn't tackle both, so he barged Danny out of the way. The lions crashed into each other and crumbled into sand.

"Thanks!" said Danny, picking

himself back up.

"It won't be long until they come back," said Jack. "We can't fight them for ever."

The ground shook, almost knocking them off their feet again. The sand that had made up the lions began to move across the ground like iron filings drawn to a magnet. They gathered together into mounds. Jack looked on in horror as more and more sand flowed from between the buildings, sucked in by an invisible force. The mound grew into a mountain, then began to take shape as a gigantic cat.

"Tigora," Jack whispered.

The giant statue was re-forming, towering taller than all the surrounding buildings. Powerful muscles bunched under the creature's flanks. Claws a metre long left deep gashes in the ground, and two feline eyes, glowing crimson with curls of black shadow, settled on Jack and Danny. Then the creature spoke, and Jack's blood froze.

"Hello, Jack. I hoped I would see you again." The voice was that of General Gore.

The shadow! Jack realised.

General Gore's spirit has taken over Tigora . . . The protector of the Leoriah is now their worst enemy!

CHAPTER 6

SUN VS SHADOW

"WHAT DO you want?" yelled Jack.

Gore's black eyes, gazing from the statue, looked up at the pyramid, where the shadows slowly crept over the surface of Solus's sun. "The Starstone will soon be mine," he said. "Once it is, I will destroy the barrier between Solus and the rest of the surface world. My shadow orb will infect the human cities as well. The earth will be plunged into endless night, and it will all belong to me."

"Nice plan!" said Danny. "But we're here to stop you."

The living statue growled. A single serrated claw extended towards Jack. "You bested me before, Chosen One, but your luck has run out. You and your puny friend cannot hope to stand against me."

"They are not alone!" said a voice from the other side of the square. Jack saw Queen Felina and several ranks of cat-people armed with spears. The queen herself clutched two metal forks ending in curved prongs like claws. "The Leoriah do not surrender to evil."

General Gore laughed. Suddenly, he swiped out a paw and raked several soldiers off their feet, throwing them high into the air. The other Leoriah threw their spears, sticking into the statue, driving Gore back. Jack felt a flare of hope, but it quickly died as the huge beast stood tall again. The spears fell from its flesh, wounds smoothing over.

"It will take more than pinpricks to fell me," said General Gore. He let out a hiss, and from several alleyways, sand lions stalked into the square.

"Spread out!" yelled Queen Felina. "Defend yourselves."

Her soldiers obeyed, and Jack hardly knew which way to look as the cat-people and the sand lions joined in frenzied battle. Soldiers were knocked down and mauled, while sand lions disintegrated into dust. Screams and growls and snarls filled the air.

"Jack, look out!" cried Danny.

Out of the corner of his eye, Jack saw something whipping towards him. Too late he realised that it was Tigora's tail.

"Ooomph!" Jack grunted as it struck him in the chest, knocking the wind from him and sending him flying. Blaze fell from his grip and he smashed into the wall of a squat building, struggling for breath. Gore leapt after him, stamping with Tigora's paws, trying to crush him. Jack rolled away, the building behind him flattened. A cloud of dust and sand blinded him for a moment, then a hand gripped his arm.

"Come on, we've got to run!" said Danny.

Jack found himself barrelling down an alleyway with his friend, and

behind he heard the thundering tread
of Tigora.

"You cannot escape!" called General
Gore.

Shooting a glance back, Jack

saw the giant cat-beast in pursuit, smashing down walls and sending innocent Leoriah running.

"I've dropped Blaze!" he shouted to Danny. "I have to go back."

"No way," said Danny. "You'll be killed!"

But Jack knew they couldn't run for ever — someone had to face General Gore and his sunsteel blade was the only weapon he knew that could defeat shadow.

"Distract him if you can," he said to Danny, then he peeled off down another alley away from his friend. He saw the great figure of Tigora streak past.

I've bought myself some time. But it won't be long before Gore tracks me down.

Jack doubled back towards the square, leaping over rubble and debris and the remains of sand lions. He knew it wouldn't be long until they re-formed. The fight between the soldiers and Gore's minions raged in the streets all around — roars and battle cries rang in the air. Jack reached the square and spotted his sword half-buried under a rock. He rushed over.

Danny's voice came through his

Oracle. "Gore's headed back your way!"

Jack was reaching for his sword when a sand lion emerged on top of the pile of rubble. It launched itself into him, knocking him on to his back. As the jaws snapped at his face, Jack punched with his super-strong hand, knocking the creature's head clean off. The rest of it collapsed on top of him in a shower of sand. Jack fought his way out from underneath, then tugged his sword free.

At the same moment he saw the statue of Tigora standing across the square, watching him.

"Just you and me now," said General Gore. "Let's finish this, 'Chosen One'."

Jack brandished Blaze with both

hands and charged. He raked the sword across one of Tigora's forelegs, and the blade sliced deep. General Gore roared in pain and collapsed.

Got you!

But the wound began to heal almost straight away, and Tigora rose once more.

"Hawk, why isn't the sunsteel hurting Gore?"

"I believe that the shadow cast by the corrupted part of the Starstone is healing him. May I suggest returning to a lighted area?"

General Gore laughed. "Your weapon is useless," he said. "We fight on my terms now."

Jack swallowed. If Blaze was ineffective, he was completely powerless.

Gore swiped with a paw, and Jack ducked. Next the tail lashed at him. Jack backed away. Gore advanced, pressing him closer to a tumbledown building at the edge of the square where there was nowhere to flee.

"I'm going to enjoy this," said the General, baring Tigora's deadly teeth. "It won't be a quick death, I'm afraid."

Jack spotted the distant pyramid over the giant cat's head. The Starstone still blazed in parts, though the section facing Leoriah was completely infected with shadow.

And then he thought of something. Perhaps there was a way to defeat General Gore. He couldn't get to a lighted area, like Hawk suggested, but maybe he could get light to come to him. "Hawk, you're a genius!" Jack cried.

"Thank you, Jack. Measured in terms of human intelligence I have an IQ of 3043."

But Jack had to get past Gore first. He sheathed his sword. "Please," he begged. "Don't hurt me!"

"Chancellor Rex was wrong about

you," said the General, chuckling. "You're no hero! I can't wait to see his face when I bring him your body."

"Hawk," whispered Jack. "Contact Ruby."

"Link with Kestrel complete."

"Ruby?" whispered Jack. "Are you still on the pyramid?"

"Jack!" said Ruby's voice. "Yes, I'm still with Ms Steel. What's going on down there?"

"I need you to use your mirror shield. Reflect light from the Starstone to me in the Leoriah city. I'll be on Tigora's pedestal."

"Ready to die?" asked General Gore.

Tigora's paw lashed out, and pinned Jack to the ground. Jack squirmed, unable to breathe. The creature's weight pressed down on him.

"Not . . . yet," choked Jack.

He reached out with both hands and grabbed the biggest rock he could find. Concentrating all his super-strength, he hurled it at Tigora's head. It struck the living statue right between its glowing eyes, and the pressure on Jack's chest vanished. Gore reeled back with a hiss. Jack punched one of the beast's legs, and the great statue collapsed forward on to its hands and knees. Jack jumped to grab on to the shoulder of the giant cat and began to haul himself up hand over hand. Gore flailed, trying to knock him off, but Jack used his super-strong hands to vault on to Tigora's back. He ran down its spine and leapt off the huge cat's tail, landing on the statue's pedestal in the centre of the square. Gore spun around to face him.

"You're only delaying your death," said the General.

"Now, Ruby!" Jack cried into his Oracle. From the top of the pyramid, a dazzling light flashed as Ruby's shield reflected the Starstone's glow towards them. Gore blinked into the glare, as if a little unsure.

But Jack raised Blaze and held the blade in the soft light. At once, the enchanted metal glowed, becoming brighter and brighter as it absorbed the Starstone's energy. Jack felt the power through the hilt in his hands.

General Gore must have realised what was happening too, for his eyes widened in alarm.

"No!" muttered the General. "I won't let you . . . "

Gore lunged, but Jack thrust out his sword at the same time. He drove the gleaming blade into the cat

statue's chest.

Gore froze and a terrible cry escaped Tigora's fanged jaws.

Cracks of light appeared across its body, snaking across its limbs. General Gore's cry rose in pitch until it was a screech, then the figure of Tigora exploded into a shower of sand and light. Jack ducked and turned from the blast, and when he looked again, there was nothing left but a ringing in his ears.

Then he heard Ruby's voice in his ear.

"Are you OK?" she asked.

"I think so," said Jack, surveying

the square below. Groups of soldiers were appearing from the side streets, looking at each other in shock, and the first few people were coming out from their houses. All that was left of the enchanted lions were heaps of sand.

Then Danny arrived across the square, a grin across his face. "You did it!" he shouted.

Jack slipped his sword into the scabbard at his side. "It isn't over yet."

• • •

A few minutes later, Jack and Danny had climbed back to the top of the pyramid. The black shadow continued to inch its way across the Starstone. As it did, Jack saw the outskirts of the scorpion city slowly falling into darkness.

"There's no way we can stop it, is there?" Jack said.

Queen Felina stood beside the med-pod, stroking her sister's brow. "Not that I know," she said. "For now, all we can do is be ready when the next city guardian is taken over by Gore's shadow."

"How long?" said Ruby.

The queen looked at them gravely. "The shadow seems to have slowed. Perhaps we have a day or two."

"We should head back to Valour Station," said Danny. "Professor Yokata needs to hear about this. At the very least, Bulk and Smarm have to be stopped before they cause more trouble."

Jack nodded. They should contact Chancellor Rex, too. But the Academy seemed a long way off at the moment. By the time Rex arrived the next statue could already be possessed with General Gore's spirit. A dark feeling crept over Jack, just like the shadow taking over the city below. He knew their oldest enemy would never rest in his quest to take over the human realm.

Jack looked at his friends, and a spark of hope flared in his heart. They would be ready. Team Hero would be ready.

TIMETABLE

	MON	TUE	WED	THUR	FRI
08.00	ASSEMBLY	ASSEMBLY	ASSEMBLY	ASSEMBLY	ASSEMBLY
09.00	POWERS	POWERS	POWERS	POWERS	POWERS
10.00	COMBAT	STRATEGY	TECH	COMBAT	STRATEGY
11.00	MATHS	GEOGRAPHY	ENGLISH	HISTORY	ENGLISH
12.00	HISTORY	SCIENCE	MATHS	SCIENCE	GEOGRAPHY
13.00	LUNCH!				
14.00	TECH	COMBAT	COMBAT	STRATEGY	WEAPON TRAINING
15.00	GYM	GYM	WEAPON TRAINING	GYM	GYM
16.00	GYM	GYM	GYM	GYM	HOMEWORK
17.00	HOMEWORK	HOMEWORK	HOMEWORK	HOMEWORK	FREE

and many from oth__
had special powers, and knew each __
once a year at a secret tournament to practise their __
skills. Each of these warriors raised their own army of
___ to do battle against the Noxxians. But Gretchen
____ strong enough to win. She wanted
____ alongside them, and she

HOMEWORK

MATHS: PAGES 25-30,
EXERCISES A-D

POWERS: TRY TO LIFT 3
TIMES OWN WEIGHT

HISTORY: REVISE FOR TEST
ON NOXXIAN WAR NEXT WEEK

TECH: WRITE A SIMPLE CODE
FOR SECURITY SENSORS

TEAM HERO ACADEMY

THE SECRET CITIES OF SOLUS

DAY: WEDNESDAY

TIME: 7.04AM

LOCATION: VALOUR STATION

JACK: Hawk?

HAWK: *Are you all right, Jack? I detect that you're out of breath and that your heart is beating unusually fast.*

JACK: Professor Yokata's early-morning combat drills wiped me out. Desert training is hard! I don't think I've ever sweated so much.

HAWK: *That explains the scent readings I'm receiving. May I suggest a shower?*

JACK: I'm on my way to the dorm now. Not that I'll be clean for long. A troop of soldiers from Solus are coming here after breakfast to spar. Professor Yokata says they'll help us prepare for whatever Gore throws at us next. But I hardly know anything about Solus and its people. And I was wondering if—

HAWK: One moment, please.

JACK: Uh . . . Hawk?

HAWK: My apologies for the delay, Jack. Information on Solus has been

made confidential by Team Hero.
However, I requested special clearance
from Chancellor Rex, which he has just
now granted. Congratulations.

JACK: Oh. Uh, thanks! So what can
you tell me?

HAWK: *The civilisation of Solus is*
truly ancient. The earliest event in their
recorded history is the Unification War
in which the races battled each other
for control of the region. Many very
dangerous weapons were used, and
the people suffered terribly.

JACK: Who won the war?

HAWK: No one. Or, put another way: everyone. The war ended when the elders of Solus's races realised that they had more similarities than differences, and understood that they could all prosper if they agreed to work together. Among the cities' leaders, a king or queen was elected to govern for the good of all Solus's people. This has proved to be an excellent solution and since then, the each city has thrived. The Leoriah are great artisans and merchants. The Avaretti are avid scholars and keep vast libraries. **The Tavnar are brilliant builders, and the Herptamon are skilled farmers and fishers. The people were much stronger together than they were apart.**

JACK: That sounds like it worked out pretty well.

HAWK: It did. Horrified by the devastation of the war, Solus's leaders sealed the most powerful weapons and artefacts from the battles in a vault that they vowed never to open. Unfortunately, soon after Unification, Solus was attacked by a ruthless enemy from the underground realms.

JACK: Noxx?

HAWK: Yes, General Gore and his armies laid siege to Solus at the same time as he assaulted the rest of the surface world. In those desperate times, Solus allied with Team Hero to fight the forces of shadow. Though Noxx was a terrible threat, the elders still feared unleashing the dangerous relics sealed within their vault, so they created a new breed of weapons using their Sunforge.

JACK: Like my sunsteel blade!

HAWK: Exactly. The skill of their

warriors, the talent of their elders and the strength of the united cities helped carry the day. However, the war gave Solus a strong desire for security from the outside world. After Gore was defeated, they broke ties with Team Hero, and created a protective magical dome to keep their existence secret from outsiders. Until very recently, it was forbidden for any Solus citizen to leave the shelter of this concealing dome. But this all changed when, for the first time in many centuries, a citizen of Solus was born with the powers of a Hero. And she wasn't born with just any ability. She had the power to teleport anywhere in the world.

JACK: Ms Steel!

HAWK: Indeed, though back then she was only known as Panthera. When Panthera discovered her ability, she began to explore the human world. From forests to mountains to our greatest cities, she was awed by the size and diversity of the outer world. Her older sister, Felina, discovered a magical ring amongst the Leoriah's treasures that could disguise Panthera as a human, so she could walk among humanity. At first, she explored in secret, but then her father, an elder of the Leoriah, discovered her. There was much concern in the council that young Panthera's adventures could put Solus in danger. With the support of Felina, Panthera reminded the council that Solus had once been allies with the humans of Team Hero, but the council wouldn't hear of it. She was forbidden from ever using her ability again.

JACK: But that's horrible! Her power is part of who she is!

HAWK: Yes, but people – whether Leoriah or Tavnar or human – often fear what they do not understand. You remember how the students in your old school did not understand your own powers.

JACK: Yeah, I'm not likely to forget. But obviously, Ms Steel — Panthera — didn't follow their orders.

HAWK: Indeed, she did not. In fact, she did something even more forbidden than leaving Solus for the human world . . . she brought someone from the human world to Solus.

JACK: The council must have been so angry! Who did she bring?

HAWK: *A young man she had befriended in her human guise. A Hero, but his ability was not to teleport, but to see the future itself.*

JACK: Chancellor Rex!

HAWK: *He was only a student at Hero Academy back then. And you're correct that the council was furious with them at first, but they changed their minds when young Rex showed them the future. That's when they learned that after a thousand years, shadow was rising once more. They understood then that all the civilisations of light* must again work together to thwart Noxx and the other evil kingdoms of the High Command.

JACK: Wow, so together Chancellor Rex and Panthera convinced them that Team Hero and Solus should be allies again?

HAWK: Yes. Panthera – Ms Steel, now – became the council's ambassador to Team Hero and took a position at Hero Academy. And Solus remained a secret to all but a select few.

JACK: It's amazing that Solus

managed to hide itself for so long time. Are there any other non-human civilisations out there?

HAWK: I see you've reached your dorm. Enjoy your shower.

JACK: Are you ignoring my question?

HAWK: If there are other secret civilisations, I'm afraid you would require additional security clearance to hear about them.

JACK: How did I know you were going to say that?

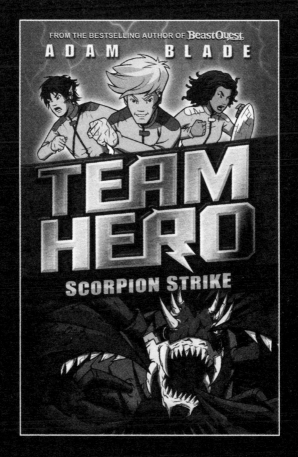

READ ON FOR A SNEAK
PEEK AT BOOK 6:

SCORPION STRIKE

CHAPTER 1

DEADLY STINGERS

JACK BOUNCED on his feet as the Tavnar captain circled him. Its insect-like jaws clacked horribly, but it was the energy stinger arching over his foe's back that Jack kept his eye on. One strike and he was finished.

Ruby shot another blast of fire from her eyes, but the Tavnar she faced quickly twisted out of the way. It already had scorch marks on its flanks, but the shell-armour worn by these scorpion warriors was tough!

Danny fired a bolt from his crossbow, and it deflected off another Tavnar's leg. The creature darted at him, smashed the crossbow aside with a pincer, then kicked Danny in the stomach. He flew through the air and landed hard on his back. Jack wanted to help, but he couldn't turn his back on his own opponent.

The Tavnar closed in on Danny.

"Here! Catch!" cried Ruby. She tossed her shield, and Danny snatched it up as an energy stinger lanced down. The mirrored steel rang out as it blocked the pulsing attack. Danny managed to roll out of the way.

"Thanks!" he said. Their three enemies regrouped too.

Above the battlefield, the Team Hero outpost of Valour Station loomed. Jack wielded his sunsteel blade — Blaze — in his scaly hand. He charged, but the scorpion warriors moved quickly, and his blows met empty air. He was sweating inside his bodysuit.

Ruby cried out, and Jack turned to see one Tavnar had trapped her against the sandy ground. As he tried to swing his sword, a pincer gripped his wrist. Another gripped his throat. He dangled, completely defenceless. Danny was pressed against the wall of Valour Station, a stinger poised right over his chest.

The Tavnar captain holding Jack grinned. "You'll have to fight better than that when Gore takes over Rachnid," she said.

She released Jack and he sagged to the ground. The other Tavnar stepped off Ruby.

"You broke my crossbow!" Danny grumbled, annoyed.

"We're not supposed to go easy on

you," said his opponent, releasing him.

Around them, the fighting continued. Professor Yokata had all available members of Team Hero sparring with their allies from the scorpion city. Working side by side with the citizens of the cities of Solus was their best chance of defeating General Gore. It would not be long until the shadow corrupting the Starstone reached Rachnid. When it did, the General would possess the statue just as he had Tigora, the cat statue which had once guarded the city of the Leoriah. Jack had defeated Gore then, but only temporarily.

"Why are you slacking?" shouted Yokata. She drifted closer on a hoverboard, frowning at them all.

"She's a tyrant!" muttered Danny.

"You might have super-hearing, but mine's just fine too," said Professor Yokata.

"Back to training!"

The Tavnar arched their stingers

and crouched low in their fighting stances. Jack readied Blaze in his hand. In a real fight, he probably could have cleaved one of the Tavnar in two if he'd used all the might of his super-strong hands. Ruby's orange eyes glowed dimly, and he knew she was only shooting her fire-beams at low power. The point of the training exercise wasn't to destroy each other, it was to stop their sparring partners from being able to fight.

"Hawk," Jack said, "do the Tavnar have any weaknesses?"

His Oracle, a kind of supercomputer attached to his ear, replied at once.

"I thought you'd never ask. Synching with Kestrel and Owl." Kestrel and Owl were Ruby and Danny's Oracles. *"Target the spot where their stingers join their tails. It's full of nerve endings. A clean strike will disable them."*

Jack saw his friends nod as Hawk's info was piped into their ears.

"Worth a try," said Ruby.

"Let's do it," said Danny.

The scorpions charged. Jack hooked his hands under Danny's foot and thrust upwards. Danny somersaulted over the Tavnar. His crossbow had been destroyed, but he held Ruby's mirrored shield ready. She sent a beam

of fire towards him. Danny adjusted
the shield, deflecting the blast down
in an arc of flame. It caught all three
on their stingers and they cried out
in pain, falling to their knees. Jack
rushed forwards and held his sword
across his opponent's neck, while

Danny landed on the back of another. Ruby sizzled the ground in front of the third — a warning shot.

"Good teamwork," said Professor Yokata.

Several others around the yard had stopped to watch and started clapping. Jack helped the Tavnar captain to her feet easily with his scaly hands. She nodded to him with new respect in her eyes.

"You got lucky," said a sneering voice. It was Olly, hovering overhead. He also wore a silver Hero Academy uniform, but his shoulder patches were green.

"Think you could do better?" asked
Danny.

Olly zipped higher. "I could have
taken all three on my own," he said.

Jack saw Ruby roll her eyes. "Why
don't you fly down here and show
us?" she said playfully.

Olly blushed. "Er . . . I told Professor
Yokata I'd train some of the others,"
he mumbled. Then he flew off.

As Jack watched him go, he saw a
woman with the face of a cat hobbling
towards them, leaning heavily on
a stick. It was Panthera, the Hero
Academy teacher he also knew as Ms
Steel. Without her enchanted ring,

her human disguise had vanished.
No more dark skin and purple hair.
They'd come to Valour Station for her
to recuperate after being captured by
Smarm and Bulk, and only learned
later that she was the sister of Queen
Felina of Solus.

"That was quite a manoeuvre you
just pulled off. It bodes well for the
coming fight against Rachnid," said
Ms Steel. Jack was pleased to see
her out of her sickbed. She seemed
to grow stronger by the hour. Gore
had infected the Starstone during a
ritual meant to heal Ms Steel from the
shadow that afflicted her. Luckily, the

magical orb's energy had cured her before Gore's evil took root within the artificial sun.

Danny returned the shield to Ruby. "I'm not sure what use I'll be," he said glumly. He tucked back his hair, and tugged his bat-like ears. "These won't fight a scorpion ten metres tall."

Ms Steel smiled. "I've met many students with many different gifts. You should trust in your powers — they might surprise you."

Check out Book Six:
SCORPION STRIKE
to find out what happens next!

IN EVERY BOOK OF
TEAM HERO SERIES
ONE there is a special
Power Token. Collect
all four tokens to get
an exclusive Team Hero
Club pack. The pack
contains everything you and
your friends need to form your
very own Team Hero Club.

MEMBERSHIP CARDS · MEMBERSHIP CERTIFICATE · STICKERS · POWER GAME · BOOKMARKS

Just fill in the form below, send it in with your four tokens
and we'll send you your Team Hero Club Pack.

SEND TO: Team Hero Club Pack Offer, Hachette Children's Books,
Marketing Department, Carmelite House, 50 Victoria Embankment,
London, EC4Y 0DZ.

CLOSING DATE: 31st December 2018

WWW.TEAMHEROBOOKS.CO.UK

Please complete using capital letters *(UK and Republic of Ireland residents only)*

FIRST NAME

SURNAME

DATE OF BIRTH

ADDRESS LINE 1

ADDRESS LINE 2

ADDRESS LINE 3

POSTCODE

PARENT OR GUARDIAN'S EMAIL

I'd like to receive Team Hero email newsletters and information about
other great Hachette Children's Group offers (I can unsubscribe at any time)

*Terms and conditions apply. For full terms and conditions please go to
teamherobooks.co.uk/terms*

*TEAM HERO Club packs
available while stocks last.
Terms and conditions apply.*

COLLECT ALL OF
SERIES TWO!

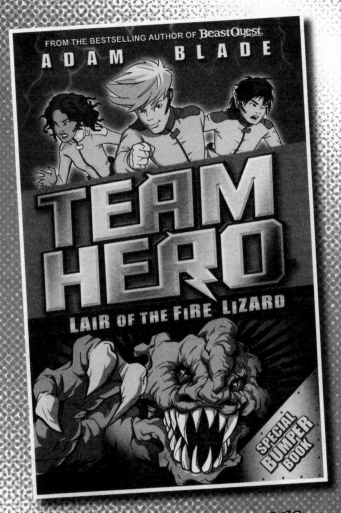

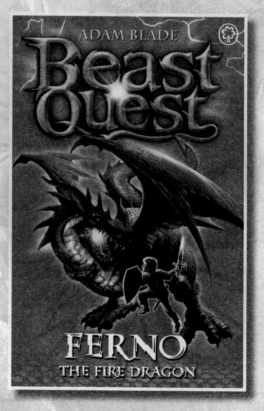

Special thanks to Michael Ford

For Jack Richardson

ORCHARD BOOKS

First published in Great Britain in 2018 by The Watts Publishing Group

1 3 5 7 9 10 8 6 4 2

Text © 2018 Beast Quest Limited
Cover and inside illustrations by Dynamo
© Beast Quest Limited 2018

Team Hero is a registered trademark in the European Union
Series created by Beast Quest Limited, London

A CIP catalogue record for this book is available from the British Library.

ISBN 978 1 40834 359 3

Printed in Great Britain

Orchard Books
An imprint of Hachette Children's Group
Part of The Watts Publishing Group Limited
Carmelite House, 50 Victoria Embankment, London EC4Y 0DZ

An Hachette UK Company
www.hachette.co.uk
www.hachettechildrens.co.uk

TEAM HERO